The Animals of Plashes Wood
Rufus the Fox

written and illustrated by Graeme Sims

FREDERICK WARNE

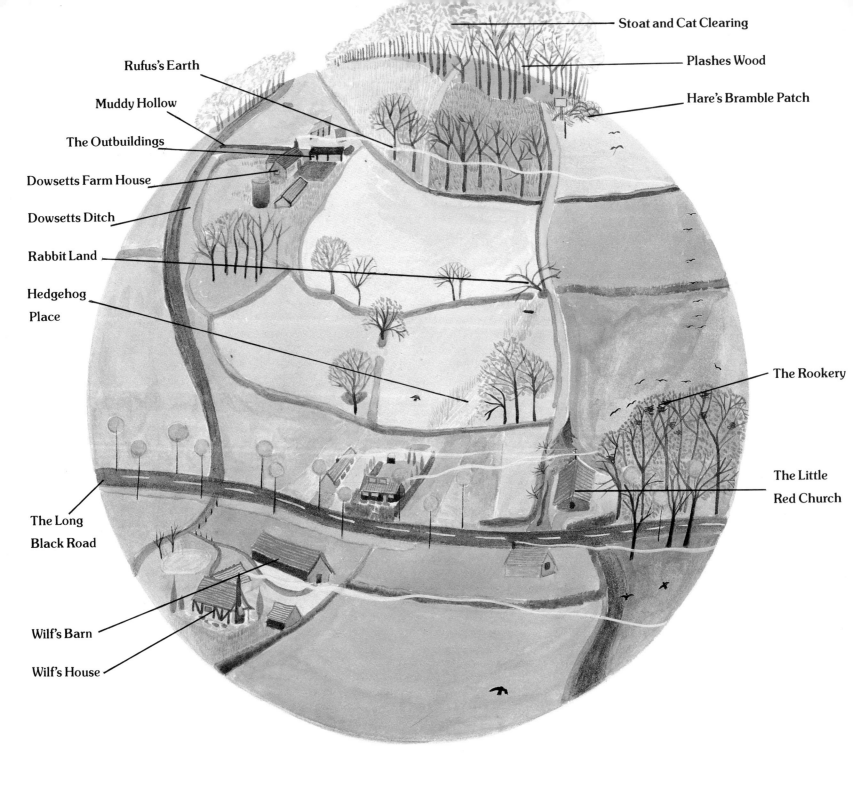

Stoat and Cat Clearing

Plashes Wood

Hare's Bramble Patch

Rufus's Earth

Muddy Hollow

The Outbuildings

Dowsetts Farm House

Dowsetts Ditch

Rabbit Land

Hedgehog Place

The Rookery

The Little Red Church

The Long Black Road

Wilf's Barn

Wilf's House

I must confess that I have always been a bit jealous of Graeme Sims. Why? Because he is both a talented artist and a very good naturalist. Now he has added authorship to his list of attributes, and all I can say is 'Great! What a superb series of books!' Each one is a collage of accurate fact, recorded both in words and pictures – wholly believable fiction *and* an accurate knowledge of both the media in which he works and the countryside in which he and his creatures live.

Open the covers, and take a look at the landscapes, from hedgehog, mouse or rabbit level, snuffle through the leaves, poke your nose or paws into the cool dark soil, meet trees root first, wander amongst the bluebells (above and below), and learn about the countryside in which you, yes *you*, live.

Plashes Wood, Flint Field and Rabbit Land are real places. What is more they are not only just around the corner from the Sims house, they are not too far away from all our homes. Even if you live in the centre of a city you can find a Plashes Wood, waiting for you to discover, only a short bus ride away.

How lucky we are, for despite its size, its population and its history, Britain is still in essence a rural country, a diversity of landscapes created by man and yet still providing habitat for many of its natural animals and birds. Unfortunately, the path of change is today very rapid and one must ask, how much longer will this happy and beautiful state of affairs continue?

If enough people read these books, take note of what they say and learn to understand their own Plashes Wood as well as Graeme and Michael Sims know theirs, the answer is forever.

DAVID BELLAMY
Bedburn

Copyright© 1983 Graeme Sims
First published in Great Britain by Frederick Warne (Publishers) Ltd, London, 1983
Book Design by Sims-Lardeaux & Co, Hertford

ISBN 0 7232 2996 1

Phototypeset by Tradespools Ltd, Frome, Somerset
Printed in Great Britain by Wm Clowes (Beccles) Ltd.

Hare sat bolt upright in a bramble thicket at the lower edge of Plashes Wood. The small hillock provided a view across the moonlit fields as far as the hills that edged the valley.

A predator was out there, and coming closer. Hare knew that it was seeking him and he trembled.

His long ears picked up the secret sounds made by the hunter and his big eyes flickered from side to side as he swept his vision across the almost daylight fields.

Rufus the Fox melted over the ground like a cloud shadow, coming closer and closer to Hare. His belly cried out for food, but at the same time he was enjoying the excitement of the chase.

For Hare, the seconds dragged out as he used all his remarkable senses in an attempt to pin-point the position of the approaching hunter.

A smoky cloud travelled across the face of the moon at the same time and a rush of wind tumbled dry leaves against the bare bramble stalks. Hare started in alarm. He put his powerful back legs into their driving position. His whole body tensed. The moment had arrived.

Rufus hurtled out of the ditch, a blurred red rush of motion, and slipped through the outer edge of the bramble thicket. He could see Hare now. He smelt the living warmth of him. Each running step cut down the distance. As Rufus made brushing contact with Hare he realised that he had missed his target. Hare leapt in the air, twisting as he went, hit the ground, and drove up the hill.

Rufus seethed, growling at his failure. It was hopeless to pursue Hare for he could run faster than any of the woodland creatures.

Life over the last few days and nights had been hard for Rufus. Men, horses and dogs had amused themselves for a whole afternoon, trying to take his life away from him. He had only avoided being torn apart by the dogs by using his brain and strength to their absolute limit. Animals seemed harder to catch these days. Some time ago he had even been outwitted by a hedgehog.

This issue now was clear—he had to find food or die. On the brow of the hill Hare thumped his big back feet against the ground in victory, and Rufus cursed.

In the distant pine forest, a little muntjac deer barked. Rufus turned his large ears towards the sound and moved on into the heart of the dark wood. He could smell Man here and all the ancestors that had gone before.

He knew that buried in the leaves of the wood, cruel metal traps were set to catch him. He kept to the footpath. There were never traps here. The animals of the wood stopped breathing and lay still in their homes. Fox was among them. Dreadful, killing, crafty Fox.

In a clearing Rufus stopped. The moon criss-crossed the open space with mysterious black shadows. An owl hooted, sending its lonely call through the dark trees. Suddenly Rufus's sharp ears picked up the sound he was waiting for. The soft whispering of leaves meant that another creature shared the clearing with him. Rufus edged silently forward. The farm cat was out hunting.

She heard Rufus breathing and froze, straining her eyes and ears for movement. As the two animals stood absolutely still, waiting for the attack, a third creature rippled over the ground towards them.

Rufus became aware of the intruder, a fraction of a second before Cat did. Here was real danger.

Two animals facing each other is normal —with three the outcome is uncertain.

Cat flattened herself against the ground, her large green eyes enlarging and her ears turning forward to pick up the slightest sound. She released her razor sharp claws from their sheaths, and nervously flicked her long tail jerkily from side to side.

Rufus stood tense and still. He bunched his muscles and waited for one of the creatures to make its move.

The third animal, noiselessly undulating over the floor of the forest, was the blood-thirsty stoat. Normally he would have picked up the scents of Fox and Cat in the air but his nose was locked—into the warm ground smell of rabbit. He relentlessly followed the scent, his senses dulled to all but his ravenous hunger for the warm furry creature.

As he drew level with Cat the lightning-fast claws ripped out and slashed the stoat across the shoulders. Startled, he dodged out of reach of the spitting Cat and ran . . . right into the jaws of Fox.

Rufus's jaws snapped shut on the neck of the rabbit hunter. Both of the surviving animals were totally alert and by now perilously close to each other. Cat was courageous, but the sight of large red Fox standing in the moonlight with the dead stoat swinging in his jaws, was too much for her.

She slowly backed away, swishing her tail and grumbling deep in her throat. She turned and pick-pawed her way towards the security of the farmyard.

Fox crossed the brow of the wooded hill and trotted down the open slope towards the fields. From a sheltered hollow beneath the twisted roots of an elm tree his mate called at his approach.

She came out of the home which they were preparing for their coming family, to lick his face.

They shared the stoat in the warmth of their earth, as the rain smacked and pattered against the wood of the tree above them.

At moments like this, life was good. They slept the day away in the safe stillness of their den.

Throughout the day the gentle spring sun warmed the earth; by night, with the coming of the cold air, the ground gave off a white mist which hung chest high. It filled the hollows of the land like snow, muffling the sounds of the night.

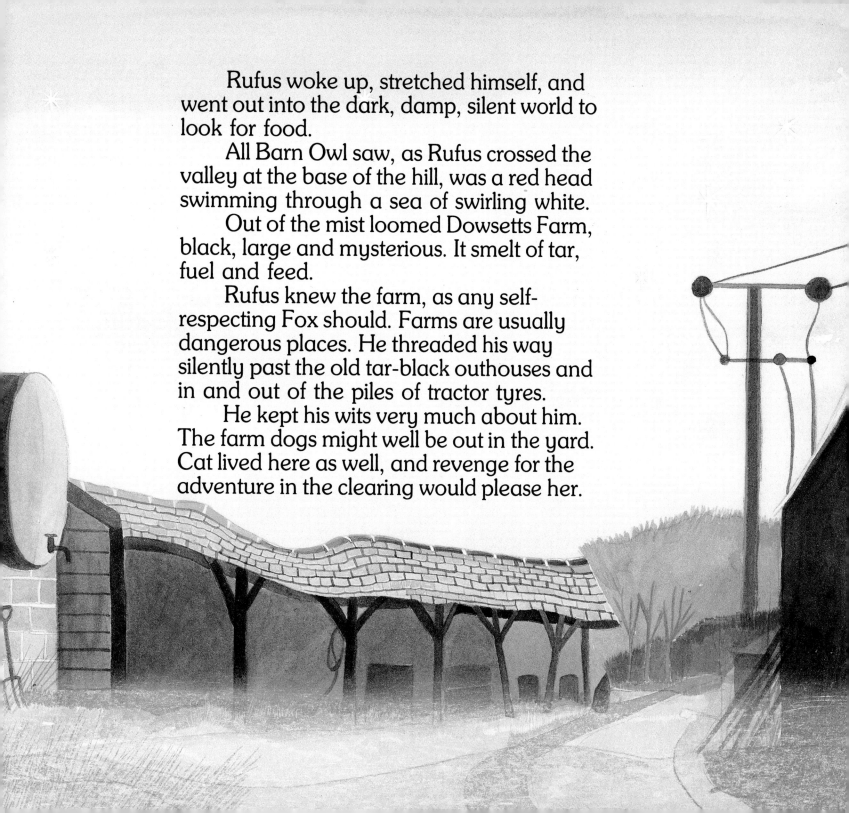

Rufus woke up, stretched himself, and went out into the dark, damp, silent world to look for food.

All Barn Owl saw, as Rufus crossed the valley at the base of the hill, was a red head swimming through a sea of swirling white.

Out of the mist loomed Dowsetts Farm, black, large and mysterious. It smelt of tar, fuel and feed.

Rufus knew the farm, as any self-respecting Fox should. Farms are usually dangerous places. He threaded his way silently past the old tar-black outhouses and in and out of the piles of tractor tyres.

He kept his wits very much about him. The farm dogs might well be out in the yard. Cat lived here as well, and revenge for the adventure in the clearing would please her.

He cautiously moved out from the shelter of the outhouses into the open space next to the farmer's house. All was misty, moist and silent.

The black glassless windows of the outbuildings stared back at Rufus like dangerous, sightless eyes.

The farm dogs could be in any one of the buildings.

He tip-toed closer to the house. No lights showed. No sound could be heard.

Near the house was a wire pen, where the farmer kept his pet pheasants.

They were already clucking nervously at Rufus's approach.

'Shush, shush, my fine beauties,' smiled Rufus soothingly. 'I'm not interested in you. You're too thin—and anyway you're quite safe in your cage. Go back to sleep,' he crooned.

The birds stopped clucking, but still eyed him warily. A chain rattled in the yard as if a sleeping dog had moved in its kennel.

Rufus paused, tense and listening. All was still again.

He crept through the mist to the kitchen window of the house—it was open just a little.

Fox stood up on his hind legs and peered through the window.

A white horse in the paddock looked up from its grazing, but made no noise.

Right in the middle of the kitchen table was a fine, fat rabbit. Fox nudged the window open, and was in and out of the kitchen with the rabbit, faster than a blink.

As his feet hit the ground of the yard one of the farm dogs barked. All at once every animal in the farm added its voice to that of the dog. The place changed from silence to uproar. Horses snorted, dogs barked, pheasants clucked, turkeys gobbled and geese hissed and cackled.

A light at the top of the house came on.

Rufus looked around in panic, but if there is one thing that foxes are good at, it is using their brains.

In a flash Rufus had run up the trellis by the side of the kitchen window, over the kitchen roof and was still and hidden in the shadow of a high chimney. Nobody would look for him there.

By now every light in the house was on. The door opened and closed with a bang. Rufus heard the farmer unchaining the dogs. Then there they all were! The dogs ran round and round the house and the farmer splashed barefoot through the cold mud of the yard, looking all about him.

The moment had come for Cat's revenge. Suddenly above him, on the next level of the roof, Rufus saw Cat's large yellow eyes. She hissed and the Farmer looked up and saw Rufus.

'I'll get my gun,' he shouted.

As he rushed into the kitchen to get his shot-gun Rufus made his way down from the roof, across the yard and into the deep ditch that ran alongside the road to the farm.

The heavy hanging mist hid him as he splashed through the water, making for the road, the fat rabbit still firmly in his jaws.

Way behind him he could hear the dogs crashing and barking around the yard.

After fifty yards or so he came up over the side of the ditch. The farmer was right behind him on the farm road, the shot-gun loaded and aimed.

All the farmer saw was a flash of red fur. There was not enough time for a clear shot. The farmer was a hard man, farmers have to be, but he was a fair one.

He would kill an animal but only if he knew he could kill it outright with one shot. He let Rufus go.

Once Rufus was sure he was out of danger his gait became more confident and he trotted across an open field, imagining the treat of the feast to come.

The poacher's shot-gun blast hit him full in the side and bowled him over in somersaults into a muddy hollow in the field . . .

When he woke up it was night again and a large full moon hung in a starry sky. His side hurt badly and he felt weak and sick. Somehow he knew that there was not much time left to him.

He stood up shakily and started to limp off across the moon-lit fields. He headed for a building that nestled in some trees at the other side of the long dark road, a mile or so from Dowsetts farm.

It was a long, painful journey that seemed to be endless.

He dragged himself weakly to the backdoor of the farmhouse. His nose picked up the familiar, friendly smells. With his last strength, he scratched at the door. Old Wilf opened it. He was dressed in his tattered tartan dressing gown, the same one that young Rufus had snuggled into as a cub. Wilf looked down at the fox. Foxes look the same to those that don't know, but Wilf knew and loved this one, for he had nursed it from a baby. Then he noticed the spreading red stain on Rufus's side.

Rufus was home. He was safe. He remembered clearly this old man's warmth and kindness, from the past.

Wilf wrapped Rufus in a blanket and carried him out to his old basket in the barn. He gently laid him down, talking softly all the time. Rufus licked his hand.

Wilf went back into the house and took his old shotgun down from above the fireplace. He hated killing but he loved Rufus too much to let him slowly die in agony. He loaded two brass-rimmed cartridges into the double-barrelled gun.

Rufus lay warm in the blanket. The pain had gone. All around him were the familiar and friendly objects of his youth. His nose picked up the smells of onion and straw. He loved this place. It was not cold, cruel and ruthless, as it was in the outside world.

He remembered nights long ago in front of the fire, snuggled up on Wilf's lap. He remembered the feel of Wilf's old hands, the warm smell of him, the way he used to continuously chatter. Then he remembered no more.

Wilf had to force himself to enter the barn, but he knew he had to do it. He walked over to the basket and bent down to pat Rufus just once more.

The handsome head lay limply over the side of the basket and the big brown eyes were blank. He knew then that the animal was dead.

Wilf stood in the yard, the loaded shotgun in his hands. The warm wind felt cold on his face. He was old, he was tired and he was desperately lonely. He remembered Rufus when he was a baby—how he used to fill the hours with his fun and mischief. He remembered the night when Rufus had gone to the kitchen door and scratched to go out.

He remembered with real sadness how Rufus had looked back at him, those big brown eyes sending a message that could not be spoken. Then Rufus had gone, to live his own life in the wild.

A single tear ran down his lined cheeks. Then in a spasm of anger he fired both barrels into the empty air.

The two gun shots merged into one barking sound and rolled in sharp echoes around the countryside.

Rufus's eldest daughter looked up at the sound and howled to the moon. Then the vixen quietly slipped like a shadow into the valley. She knew that a hare waited for her in a bramble thicket on the edge of Plashes Wood.